The Inside Outing

Elizabeth Laird and Olivia Madden
Pictures by Deborah Ward

Barron's
New York • Toronto

First edition for the United States, Canada, and the Philippines published 1988
by Barron's Educational Series, Inc. 250 Wireless Boulevard.
Hauppauge, New York 11788

First published in 1987 by William Heinemann Ltd., London, England.

Library of Congress Catalog Card No. 88-7036

International Standard Book No. 0-8120-5977-8

Printed by Mandarin Offset in Hong Kong
890   987654321

Julie woke up feeling excited. She was going
to the beach with her friends.
She climbed down from her bunkbed very quietly.
She didn't want to wake her baby sister Kate.

Julie looked out of the kitchen window.
"We won't be able to go now!" she said miserably.
"Never mind," said Mom. "We'll invite your
friends to come here instead."

"But what about our picnic?" asked Julie.
"You can have it here," said Mom.
   That gave Julie a good idea.
"I know what we'll do," she said.
"We'll play going to the beach at home."

Soon Julie's friends arrived.

Ben was carrying a bag full of beach things.

"It's a pity about the rain," said Amy.

"It doesn't matter," said Julie.

"What do you mean?" asked William.

"Come up to my bedroom," said Julie.

"It's a surprise."

"Your bed!" said Ben. "It's turned into a boat!
    And here's the sea, and the beach!"
"Can we go on board?" asked Amy.
"We'll have to dress up first," said William, and he
    pulled his pirate hat out of the bag.

"I'll just fix up the
sail," said Julie.

"And I'll make a flag,"
said William.

"This is the gang
plank," said Ben.

"And here are the
tickets," said Amy.

"The top bunk's the deck," said Julie, "and the
   cabins are below."
"We'll need a wheel to steer with," said Ben.
"I don't want to get blown out to sea."
"Here's just the thing," said William.

At last the ship was ready.
"All aboard!" said Julie.
"Tickets please."

"It's an ocean liner," said Amy. "I'm in the cabin."
"No it isn't, it's a pirate ship," said William,
  frowning fiercely up on deck.
"No fighting among the crew," said Julie.
"Pull in the anchor! We're off!"

"Whew! I'm hot!" said Ben after a while, and he took
  off his sweater.
"Me, too," said William, and he took off his hat.
"Man overboard!" shouted Amy suddenly. "Kate's
  fallen into the sea!"

One after another, the children jumped off the boat.
"This is fun," said Julie, splashing about.
"I'm doing the backstroke," said Ben.
"Quick!" shouted William. "Get back on board!
There's a terrible storm blowing up!"

"Batten down the hatches!" called Julie, slipping under the bedclothes.
Amy pulled the curtains across.
"We'll be safe in here," she said to Kate.

"We'll be blown onto the rocks!" shouted Ben.
"Pull in the sail!"
"I'll be the lookout," said William.
"Land ahead!" he said. "We're saved!"
"And about time too," said Amy. "Kate's been
    seasick all over my legs."

"We've arrived at an island," announced Ben.
"Let's go ashore in the rowboat and explore."

"Here's our tent," said Julie,
getting down to work.

"And here's a palm tree,"
said Ben, "for shade."

"Here's the fire," said William,
"to keep the lions away."

"We're going wading," said Amy,
holding up her skirt.

Soon it was lunchtime.
The children ran downstairs to the kitchen.
"Can we make a seaside restaurant, Mom?"
asked Julie.
"All right," said Mom, "if you do the work."

Ben made a big sign
and pinned it up.

Amy made menus
for everyone.

Julie made crab platters
and banana seaweed.

And William kept an
eye on Kate.

When lunch was ready, they all lined up.
"No pushing at the back there," said Julie.
"I want two of those banana puddings," said William.
"I'm desperate for a drink," said Ben. "Sailing always makes me thirsty."

They sat down at the table.
"Pass the cookies please," said Amy.
"Cherries! Cherries!" said Kate.
"No more, dear," said Mom. "You'll be sick."
"I'm tired," said Julie, when they had finished.
"Let's go and sunbathe on the beach now."

Julie laid out a towel for everyone to lie on.
Amy made paper sunhats.
"Don't you go and eat yours, Kate," she said.
Ben set up an umbrella.
"We don't want to get too sunburned," he said.
William was putting up a red flag. "That means
it's too dangerous to swim," he said.

The children changed into their bathing suits.
"This is the life," said Julie.
"I'm burying my hands in the sand," said Ben,
   pushing his fingers under the cushion.
"What's that?" asked Amy, sitting up with a jerk.
"Only a spider, my dear," said William.
   Kate said nothing at all. She was fast asleep.

Soon, everyone got bored with sunbathing.
"Let's go beachcombing," said William.
"There's lots of fishy stuff around this island."
Amy found a long sock. "Ugh! An eel!" she said.
Ben found a sheriff's badge. "A starfish!"
he said. "Hooray!"
Julie found a long green scarf.
"Seaweed!" she said. "Just the thing."
William found a paper boat.
"Let's make some more of these, and have
a race in the bathtub," he said.

It didn't take long to make the boats.
When they were ready, the children climbed into
their rowboat, and rowed to the bathroom.
"Wait for Kate," said Julie. "She's awake again."

Ben ran some cold water in the tub. He was careful
not to fill it up too much.
The children put their boats in a line at one side,
and blew them across to the other.
Julie won the first race, and William won the second.
"Never mind, Amy," said Ben.
"Let's go back to the beach."

"This ocean needs a bit of wildlife," said Amy.
"I'm going to make some fish."
"There should be seagulls, too," said Ben.
"I'm going to make a mobile."

"You'll have to watch out," said Julie.
"There's a giant octopus in these waters."
"Worse than that," said William.
"The sea's infested with sharks."

"Time's nearly up," said Julie. "We'd better get back on board."

"Into the rowboat, Kate," said Amy. "You don't want to get eaten by sharks."

"I'll keep a lookout for you," said Ben.

"I've made myself a pair of binoculars."

"We're off!" shouted Julie. "Homeward bound!"
"Goodbye, beautiful island!" shouted Amy.
"Pull up the anchor!" shouted Ben.
"Hey! A shark's trying to chew the chain in half!"

It was time to go home.

"Did you enjoy yourselves?" asked Mom.

"It was wonderful," said Ben.

"Fabulous," said William. "As good as the real beach any day."